Usborne First Stories
LITTLE RED RIDING HOOD

Retold by Heather Amery
Illustrated by Stephen Cartwright

Language Consultant: Betty Root
Reading and Language Information Centre
University of Reading, England

There is a little yellow duck to find on every page.

Once upon a time, there was a little girl who lived with her Mother on the edge of a big, dark forest. The little girl's Grandmother made her a bright red cloak with a hood, so everyone called her Little Red Riding Hood.

One day her mother said, "Your Grandmother is ill. I'll put some food in a basket and you can take it to her. Go along the forest path to her cottage but, remember, don't talk to any strangers you meet on the way."

Little Red Riding Hood waved goodbye to her
Mother and went into the forest with the basket.

It was such a lovely day, she sang a little song as
she skipped along the path. She did not see a big
grey Wolf watching her from behind a tree.

Suddenly the Wolf jumped out in front of her. Little Red Riding Hood was frightened but the Wolf smiled. "Where are you going, little girl?" he said. "I'm taking this basket of food to my Granny who lives in a cottage in the forest," she said.

The Wolf smiled a wicked smile. "Why not pick some of these pretty flowers for her?" he said. Little Red Riding Hood did not like the Wolf's smile but she thought her Grandmother would like some flowers. "That's a good idea, Mr Wolf," she said.

She put down her basket and started to pick a big
bunch of flowers. The Wolf smiled again, showing
all his sharp white teeth. Then he ran silently down
the path to find Grandmother's cottage. He was
very, very hungry.

The Wolf found the cottage and looked in through the window. Grandmother was sitting up in bed.

He knocked on the door. "Come in," she called. The Wolf opened the door and ran in. Quick as a flash he gobbled her up in one great gulp.

Then he climbed into Grandmother's bed, and put on her night cap and glasses. He pulled the bed clothes right up to his chin, lay back on the pillows and waited for Little Red Riding Hood to come in.

When Little Red Riding Hood reached
Grandmother's cottage with her basket of food and
bunch of flowers, she knocked on the door. "Come
in, my dear," called the Wolf in a squeaky voice.
"I'm in my bedroom."

Little Red Riding Hood went in. "Hello, Granny,"
she said, "I've brought you some food and some
flowers." Then she stared and stared. "But,
Granny," she said, "what big eyes you've got."
"All the better to see you with," said the Wolf.

"But, Granny," said Little Red Riding Hood,
feeling a bit frightened, "what big ears you've got."
"All the better to hear you with," said the Wolf.
"But, Granny," said Little Red Riding Hood, feeling
very frightened, "what big teeth you've got."

"All the better to eat you with," growled the Wolf.
And he jumped out of bed. Little Red Riding Hood
screamed but the Wolf gobbled her up in one great
gulp. Then he climbed slowly back into bed, gave a
great yawn and fell asleep.

Out in the forest, a Woodman heard the scream from the cottage. "I wonder what that was," he said. "I'd better see if the old lady is all right."

He ran to the cottage, in through the open door and straight into Grandmother's bedroom.

When he saw the Wolf asleep in Grandmother's bed, he killed it with one blow of his axe. Then he slit open its stomach with his knife. Inside were Little Red Riding Hood and her Grandmother, a bit squashed but alive and very happy to be rescued.

"Thank you very much for saving us from the wicked Wolf," said Grandmother. The Woodman dragged the dead Wolf out of the cottage and they all sat down to a delicious meal.

First published in 1987. Usborne Publishing Ltd, 83-85 Saffron Hill, London EC1N 8RT, England. © Usborne Publishing Ltd, 1987